There is a yellow breakdown truck
And Benny is his name.
He works at Smallbills Garage,
And breakdowns are his game.

Benny the Breakdown Truck

Mike McCannick

Alfie Romeo

Carmen Gear

Francis Ford Popular

Morton

Warren Beetle

Doris Minor

BENNY
The Breakdown Truck
Five Stories from Smallbills Garage

Keren Ludlow and Willy Smax

Imo the Limo

Crown Publishers, Inc., New York

For Jamie

Published by Crown Publishers, Inc., a Random House company,

201 East 50th Street, New York, New York 10022.

Originally published in Great Britain in 1994 by Orion Children's Books, London.

CROWN is a trademark of Crown Publishers, Inc.

Manufactured in Italy

Library of Congress Cataloging-in-Publication Data

Smax, Willy.

Benny the Breakdown Truck / by Willy Smax ; illustrated by Keren Ludlow.

p. cm.

Summary: Benny, a kindly tow truck, helps out other cars and trucks.

[1. Trucks—Fiction. 2. Cars   Fiction.] I. Ludlow, Keren, ill II Title.

PZ7.S63934Be 1994

[E]—dc20   93-50048

ISBN 0-517-59921-X

10 9 8 7 6 5 4 3 2 1

First American Edition

Tool Trouble at Smallbills Garage

Benny the Breakdown Truck was watching Mike McCannick at work in Smallbills Garage.

There were lots of cars to be repaired, and Mike was rushing around trying to get them all fixed.

"Don't forget to check my brakes, young man," said Doris Minor.

"And while you're
changing my oil,"
said Warren Beetle,
who was up on the lift,
"you can adjust my clutch."

"Look at the mess he's making,"
said Francis Ford Popular as Mike searched for the
right wrench.

For once Benny had to agree with Mike's snooty
old black car.

"Yes," he said, "and it seems to be getting
worse."

Alfie Romeo, the bright red sports car, was feeling impatient.

"Hurry up, please," he said to Mike. "My carburetor is killing me."

"I'll be with you in a minute," said Mike, hunting around for his screwdriver.

Suddenly he tripped over the wheel wrench and fell backward over some oil cans.

Mike's tools were scattered all over the floor. He couldn't find anything.

"Oh, dear," he said. "How can I ever get finished now?" He sat down sadly on an oil can and stared at the mess.

Francis Ford Popular looked snootier than ever.

"I shouldn't have to put up with this," he said. "It's like living in a junkyard."

"You've just given me an idea," said Benny. And he drove out of the garage and down the road to Brummingham.

By now the cars were all starting to complain.

"I can't wait here all day with my hood up," said Alfie.

"I'm getting dizzy up on this lift," said Warren.

"Please hurry up," said Doris Minor. "I'm getting awful twinges in my universal joints."

Poor Mike didn't know what to do. He looked around the garage and noticed that Benny was missing.

"Where's Benny?" he asked Francis.

"Here he comes now," said Francis. "And what on earth has he got with him?"

Hanging from Benny's towing hook was a huge round metal object.

"Where have you been?" asked Mike.

"I went to the junkyard to borrow their giant magnet," said Benny. "Watch this!"

Benny lowered the big magnet. As if by magic, the tools began to roll across the floor. Then they jumped up and stuck to the magnet.

"Oh, look!" said Mike. "There's my screwdriver! And there's my monkey wrench!"

Benny swung the big magnet around the garage until the floor was clear. With all Mike's tools sticking to it, the magnet looked like an enormous porcupine.

"Thanks, Benny!" said Mike.
"Now that I can see my tools,
I'll be finished in no time."

He tightened up Doris's
lug nuts. Then he reached
for his screwdriver and
adjusted Warren's clutch.

Soon Mike had fixed Alfie's carburetor. Smallbills
Garage was peaceful again.

"That's better," said Francis, looking at all the tools sticking to the magnet. "I hate living in a mess."

"Well, now the tools are just like you," said Benny.

"Because they're clean and tidy?" asked Francis.

"No," said Benny. "Because they're stuck up!"

The End

Doris Minor's Parking Space

Doris Minor was a very old car. You could tell because she had old-fashioned turn signals that moved up and down.

One day she was shopping on the high street. It was very crowded because road rollers and front-end loaders were repairing the road.

"Oh, good!" said Doris. "There's a parking space." And she began to back into it.

But a big blue car tried to back in first.

"Look out, slowpoke!" he shouted.

Doris couldn't stop in time. BANG! The two cars crashed together, and poor Doris bent her rear fender.

"OW!" she cried. "Now look at what you've done!"

"I was here first," said the big blue car. "You'll have to go somewhere else."

BEEP!

BEEP!

BEEP!

HONK!

HONK!

BEEP!

But Doris was stuck.
Her fender was bent against
her tire, and she couldn't move.

The cars around her started to
honk their horns.

"BEEP! BEEP! Move out of the way!"

Benny the Breakdown Truck and Mike
McCannick were driving by. They wondered
what all the noise was about. Benny stopped
and asked Doris what was wrong.

"That rude car bent my fender when he took
my parking space," said Doris. "Now I'm stuck."
"I'll soon fix that," said Mike. He jumped out
of the cab with his toolbox and began to
mend the damage.

Benny turned on his flashing orange lights
to warn the other cars about the accident.
He looked down at the bad blue car
and said, "Fancy taking an old lady's
parking space! You'd better go and
park somewhere else."

23

The blue car looked up at the big yellow breakdown truck and decided he'd better move. He saw a space on the other side of the street and started to back into it.

"You can't park there," said Benny. "That's where they're repairing the road."

"So what?" said the blue car. He bumped the
traffic cones out of the way and parked between a
road roller and a huge truck full of macadam.

Mike levered Doris's fender straight, and she
drove into her parking space.

"Thank you so much, young man," she said.

Suddenly there was a commotion across the street.

The truck full of macadam had turned on its hydraulic dumper. It didn't know that anyone had parked behind it.

"STOP!" the blue car shouted, but it
was too late. The dump truck's
tailgate swung open, and macadam
poured out all over the blue car.

WHOOSH!

Soon all that could be seen was a
pair of headlights poking out of a
mountain of macadam.
"Get me out of here!" came a muffled cry.

"I think we'd better lend a hand," said Mike to Benny.

By this time a crowd had gathered to see what was going on. They all roared with laughter as Benny towed the blue car home, leaving a long trail of macadam behind it.

Benny the Big Star

"Come on, Benny!" said Mike. "We've got to pick up Mr. Bergspiel's limousine."

"Not *the* Mr. Bergspiel, the film director?" said Benny.

"That's the one," said Mike.

"Wow!" said Benny.

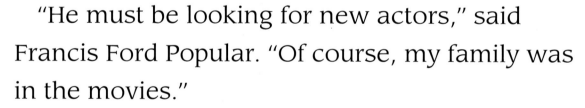

"He must be looking for new actors," said Francis Ford Popular. "Of course, my family was in the movies."

"Yes, wasn't your grandfather a moving van?" said Benny.

"You'll laugh out of the other side of your radiator when I star in Mr. Bergspiel's next film," said Francis.

Benny drove out through the automatic doors and stopped at the traffic light next to Warren Beetle, the vainest car in Brummingham.

"Where are you going?" asked Warren, admiring his reflection in Benny's big hubcap.

"I'm going to pick up Mr. Bergspiel's limousine," said Benny proudly.

"Mr. Bergspiel, the film director?" said Warren excitedly. "I must rush. I've got to go to the car wash." And off he sped.

Benny and Mike found a long black car with tinted windows parked across three parking meters.

"Are you Imogene the limousine?" asked Mike.

"Yeah," said the long black car, "but most people call me Imo the Limo."

Mike hooked up Imo to Benny's towing bar, and he towed her back to Smallbills Garage.

Mike began to work underneath Imo.

"Is Mr. Bergspiel really here to find cars for his new film?" asked Benny.

"He sure is," said the long black car. "Right now we're looking for a getaway car."

Just then Warren Beetle drove up, wearing a big blue visor and gleaming with wax.

"Hi," drawled Warren, flashing his headlights at Imo the Limo. "New in town?"

"Yeah," said the limousine.

"What line of business are you in?" asked Warren, as if he didn't already know.

"I'm in the film business," said Imo.

"Oh, really?" said Warren. "What a coincidence. I'm an actor myself." And he turned around to show off his best side.

Then Francis Ford Popular rolled up.
"I couldn't help overhearing that you're looking for actors. Allow me to introduce myself: Francis Ford Popular III."

"Pleased to meet you," said Imo. "I suppose you're an actor too." "How clever of you to notice," said Francis. "Acting is in my oil, you know."

Mike slid out from underneath Imo's engine.

"Okay," he said. "Try it now."

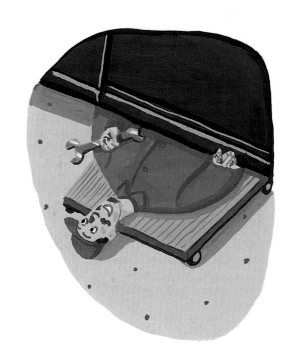

Imo turned on her ignition, and the engine started the first time.

"The boss will be happy," said Imo.

Mr. Bergspiel was very pleased indeed. He opened the tinted rear window and thanked Mike. Then he asked about hiring a getaway car from him.

Warren and Francis waited impatiently while Mike talked to the film director.

"Which one of us does he want?" they asked when Mike came back into the garage.

"Neither of you two," said Mike. "Mr. Bergspiel says that Benny is the only one in town tough enough for the part."

Benny's headlights beamed. "Yippee!" he yelled.

All Warren and Francis could do was stand and stare as Benny followed Imo the Limo out to the film set.

"I've never liked his films anyway," said Warren Beetle when they had all gone.

"Me neither," said Francis Ford Popular. And they moaned on and on until Mike came back to lock up the garage.

Morton Goes Flying

Morton the naughty blue motorcycle was sitting in the sun outside Smallbills Garage when the parts deliveryman arrived.

He was carrying so many boxes of spark plugs he could hardly see where he was going.

I'll give him a shock, thought naughty Morton.
"BEEP!" He honked his horn as loud as he
could.

The poor deliveryman nearly jumped out of
his socks with fright. All his boxes went
flying through the air. Mike McCannick
came out of the garage to see what was
going on.

"Morton!" scolded Mike. "What are you doing?
I told you to sit still and keep quiet. You'd better
not be naughty again. If you move an inch, I'll
take your wheels off for a week."

Morton tried to sit quietly, but he soon got bored. He began to rock back and forth on his stand. Suddenly he saw Alfie Romeo zooming past.

"Can't catch me!" yelled the red sports car.

"We'll see about that," said Morton, and with a twist of his throttle, he raced down the road. He roared

VROOM! in first gear,

BRUM! into second gear,

and NEEOWWM! into third gear.

Alfie Romeo looked in his rearview mirror. Here comes Morton, he thought, but he'll never catch me! And he passed a bus, a truck, and three cars in one move.

"Watch this," said Morton, and he VROOMED! into fourth gear and BRUMMED! into fifth. "Wheeee! I'm catching up!"

Alfie Romeo slowed down for the canal bridge corner.

"NOW I'll catch him!" said Morton, speeding up around the bend. But he was going so fast he couldn't slow down for the bridge. As soon as he hit it, he took off.

"I'm flying!" yelled Morton.

He sailed through the air toward a big truck. It was Farmer Pajama, driving a huge load of manure up to Bedstead Farm.

"OOOHHH!" screamed Morton as he landed SPLUDOOP! right in the middle of it.

He sank down, going PLUP, PLUP, PLUP, all the way to the bottom.

Farmer Pajama didn't even notice. When he reached Bedstead Farm, he tipped up the back of the truck and poured the manure onto the ground. He watched in surprise as a dark shape slipped out. Morton hit the concrete so hard that his mirror fell off.

Farmer Pajama turned on the hose to see what it was.

"It's Morton the naughty blue motorcycle!" he said. "How did YOU get here?"

"I was just passing and I thought I'd drop in," said Morton.

"Well, you can just drop out again," said Farmer Pajama. "This is pure manure, and it doesn't need a mucky old motorcycle messing it up."

Morton had never smelled anything so bad in his life. He shot off, trying to get home without anyone noticing. But there was a traffic jam, and he had to thread his way slowly between the cars and trucks.

"UGH!" said Warren Beetle. "What's that smell?"

A big yellow cement mixer sounded his horn. "HONK, HONK, what a STINK!"

Morton got back to Smallbills Garage just as Mike was closing the automatic doors. He parked and tried to pretend that nothing had happened.

"Hello, Morton," said Mike, "did you have a nice rest? Ugh . . . what's that smell?"

"What smell?" said Morton, pretending he couldn't smell anything.

"And where's your mirror?" said Mike, holding his nose.

"Here it is," said Farmer Pajama, who had just walked up. "It must have broken off when he fell out of my muck truck."

"That does it! Now I really am going to take your wheels off," said Mike. "Where's my wrench?"

"Here," said Farmer Pajama, "please use mine."

And Morton didn't go out for a week.

The End

Alfie Makes a Splash

Mike McCannick walked into Smallbills Garage carrying a large can of 20/50 motor oil.

"Yum, yum!" said Benny. "My favorite."

"Sorry, Benny, but it's not for you," said Mike. "It's for Roland Royce. He's coming in for a tune-up."

"I never get anything nice," grumbled Benny.

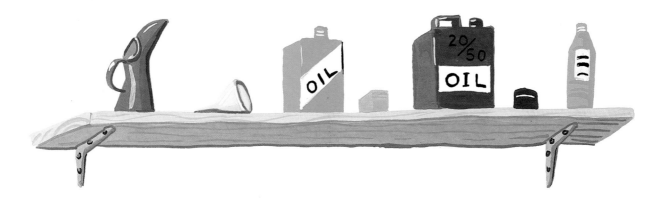

"That's because you're a dirty old breakdown truck," said Francis Ford Popular. "Expensive oil is only for posh cars like Roland Royce and me."

"If you're posh, then I'm a pushcart," said Benny.

"That's enough, you two," said Mike. "Time for work, Benny. We've got to pick up some parts for Roland."

They drove off to the car parts store.

"Oh-oh!" said Mike, looking in his rearview mirror. "Look who's coming up behind us."

It was Alfie Romeo, flashing his lights to pass. "You're not chasing Carmen again, are you?" asked Benny when they stopped together at the next intersection.

"Yes," said Alfie, "and I would have caught her by now if you weren't blocking the road!"

"Pardon me for brumming!" said Benny.

He and Mike watched as Alfie shot out through a small gap in the traffic, nearly causing an accident.

But Alfie had to stop at the traffic light, and Carmen turned left over the canal bridge.

"She's got away," said Benny, pulling up next to Alfie again.

"Oh, shut up and move over," said Alfie. "I'm going to take a shortcut."

"Hey! Don't go down there!" shouted Benny. "It's—"

Alfie didn't wait to listen. He shot off down a ramp, going so fast he didn't see that it went straight down to the canal.

There was a huge SPLASH as Alfie hit the water.

"Help! Help!" he shouted. "I'm drowning!"
"Oh, no!" said Mike. "Alfie's fallen in!"

Benny had a bright idea. He whizzed down the
road, turned onto the bridge, and backed up to
the railing.

He lowered his big hook so that it caught
under Alfie's bumper and pulled him up,
dripping with water, through the air.

A crowd had gathered,
and everyone cheered as
Benny lifted Alfie over
the railing. Then Benny
proudly towed Alfie home.

Back at the garage, Mike cleaned out Alfie Romeo's carburetor and recharged his battery. By the end of the day, Alfie was feeling fine.

"I'm sorry I was rude to you, Benny," said Alfie. "Thank you for saving my life."

"That's okay," said Benny. "That's my job."

"Benny, I think you deserve a reward," said Mike, and he picked up the big can of 20/50 motor oil. Slowly he poured the thick golden oil into Benny's engine.

Francis Ford Popular couldn't believe his headlights when he saw Benny glugging down Roland Royce's favorite drink.

"But that's only for posh cars like me and Roland," he said.

"Posh cars—and heroes," said Alfie Romeo.

"That's right," said Mike, getting ready to go home. "Good night, Benny! Good night, Alfie!" He looked over to Francis. "And good night to you, your royal highness."

If you break down in Brummingham,
You'll know that you're in luck,
If you're towed to Smallbills Garage
By Benny the Breakdown Truck.